To Nicole Mandrell Shipley,
an answer to a mother's prayers.
And to Clint and Rance Collins,
the godchildren who have
blessed my life beyond compare.
LOUISE

For my sons, Clint and Rance,
who have taught me that
a parent's smiles and tears
are the most precious
of all of God's gifts.
ACE

To all the children
who will touch this book,
may your childhood
be filled with love.
LOUISE AND ACE

A Mission For Jenny

A Mission

Louise Mandrell and Ace Collins

Children's Holiday Adventure Series
Volume 9

THE SUMMIT GROUP

1227 West Magnolia, Suite 500, Fort Worth, Texas 76104

© 1993 by Louise Mandrell and Ace Collins. All rights reserved.

All rights reserved. Published 1993.

Printed in the United States of America.

93   10   9   8   7   6   5   4   3   2   1

Jacket and Book Design by Cheryl Corbitt

LIBRARY OF CONGRESS CATALOGING-IN-PUBLICATION DATA

Mandrell, Louise.

   A mission for Jenny / Louise Mandrell and Ace Collins; illustrated by Leslie Stall.

   p. cm. – (Louise Mandrell & Ace Collins holiday adventure series; v. 9)

   Summary: In 1776, early in the American Revolution, nine-year old Jenny is befriended in
Philadelphia by a future president and meets a woman who will become a legend.

   ISBN 1-56530-038-6: $12.95

   1. United States – History – Revolution, 1775-1776 – Juvenile fiction. [1. United States –
History – Revolution, 1775-1783 – Fiction. 2. Philadelphia – Fiction. 3. Ross, Betsy, 1752-1836 –
Fiction. 4. Washington, George, 1732-1799 – Fiction.] I. Collins, Ace. II. Stall, Leslie, ill. III.
Title. IV. Series: Mandrell, Louise. Louise Mandrell & Ace Collins holiday adventure series; v. 9.

PZ7. M31254Mi   1993

[Fic] – dc20   93-299

CIP

AC

For Jenny

Illustrated by Leslie Stall

THE SUMMIT GROUP

"Jennifer!"

Mary Stuart's voice called out across the backyard and down the long, brick-covered alley that ran behind it. "Jennifer Stuart, it is time for you to come home!"

Hearing the urgency in her mother's voice, nine-year-old Jenny jumped up from the bench beside her neighbor's blooming rose bushes. Grabbing a doll made of old rags, she clutched it in her arms and said, "Elizabeth, she sounds like she means it! We'd better run home quick!" Tucking the doll under her arm, she raced out the back gate and into the alley. Within minutes, she was at her own back door.

"Where have you been?" asked her mother in an exasperated tone. Before Jenny could answer, she added, "You'd better wash your hands. It's time to take your father his lunch. He'll be expecting you any minute."

A few minutes later, after she had tucked Elizabeth safely into a homemade doll's bed, Jenny skipped out the front door of her white clapboard house and emerged once more into the bright light of a midsummer day. In her hand she carried a covered basket which held the lunch that her mother had packed for her father. But before she could give his meal to him, she would have to walk almost a mile through some of Philadelphia's busiest streets.

It was a time when the country was in an uproar. The year was 1776, and talk of freedom filled almost every conversation, newspaper, and church sermon. As Jenny walked by the park, she overheard the old men on benches speaking of war and wondering out loud if General Washington and his army had a chance against the British. Many of them didn't seem very hopeful. The army from across the sea certainly did look big and tough compared to the ragtag bunch of rebels who had joined the united colonies' cause.

Jenny listened without giving much thought to what the men were saying. Nor did she give much thought to a war that was raging in towns that seemed so far away. But she knew that her father supported General Washington and the fight for freedom. At the supper table he often read the words Mr. Benjamin Franklin wrote in that day's paper. And when her father mentioned Mr. Franklin's name, Jenny took notice. She had met him once. She had thought of him as a funny old man, kind of round and jolly, like a big pumpkin with a white wig and glasses. He had been nice to her, complimenting her on her pink dress and big brown eyes, so she figured that, beneath the funny, mugging face, he must be a pretty smart man. Still, she didn't see what fighting the British and King George had to do with her own life in Philadelphia. What could she do about any of it anyway? It seemed to be a business for grown-ups.

As she marched down the cobblestone street, she stopped now and then to admire one of the city's wealthy families as they passed in their elegant, horsedrawn carriages. Wouldn't it be nice, she thought, to be so important as those people? It would be so much fun to be able to do whatever you wanted, to go wherever you wanted, and to buy everything you saw. As each carriage passed out of sight, she continued her walk, all the time picturing herself as a very important person.

About a block from her father's shop, she noticed that a crowd had gathered. Pushing her way to the front, she watched as a man in a fancy blue uniform, three-cornered hat, and polished boots gave a speech. He talked of loyalty and service, and everyone hung on his words. Then, as he mounted a large, white horse, the crowd cheered, the men raising their hats in salute. Jenny cheered too, even though she had no idea who the man was or why she was cheering. "Why can't I ever do anything important?" she said to herself. "Why do people who make a difference always have to be grown-ups?"

Then, remembering her errand, she hurried on down the street to her father's shop. She liked visiting her father at his shop. And while he ate, she could wander around his displays of fine materials. Maybe her father would let her take a piece home to make Elizabeth a new dress.

Ethan Stuart's shop was in a two-story, red-brick building. In the windows were displays of the newest materials from the Far East. These items would tempt many buyers, but they cost far too much for anyone except the very rich. The simpler cotton and wool goods may not have been in the window, but these fabrics were the ones that Jenny's father kept in the largest quantities. They were the items most needed and purchased most often by his customers.

As Jenny opened the shop's heavy, oak door, the smell of freshly opened packages of cloth greeted her. It was a smell with which she had grown up. Selling dry goods had been the business of her grandfather even before it was her father's, and some of Jenny's first memories were of brightly colored cloth and spools of thread. To her, it didn't seem like an important job, and it certainly didn't make the Stuarts one of the city's important families, but at least it gave her a chance to use scraps to make dresses for Elizabeth.

"Jenny," Ethan Stuart's deep voice called out as she walked in, "I had begun to wonder if your mother had forgotten my lunch!"

"Hello, Father," Jenny called out happily. Marching over to a large counter covered with layers of cloth, she handed her father his lunch. While he unpacked the small basket, she took inventory of all the colors that lay before her. As she wandered about the shop, her father sat back in his cane-bottomed, high-backed wooden chair and eagerly ate two pieces of homemade bread, an apple, and a piece of dried pork. Washing it down with water, he smiled, wiped his mouth with a handkerchief, and then returned to the counter.

"Where's Mr. Evans?" Jenny asked, realizing that her father's assistant was not in the shop.

"He went home ill today," her father explained. "I think he has caught a summer cold. He wanted to work, but I told him to get some rest. He should be back tomorrow."

Ethan Stuart observed his daughter as she examined each roll of fabric. He watched her study a blue and pink striped pattern for several minutes, carefully touching it, letting her mind imagine what it would look like on Elizabeth. Then, before she could move on to the next pattern, he asked, "Do you like it?"

"It is beautiful," she answered enthusiastically.

"I think I know a way that you could earn a small piece of it, if you are willing to do something special for me." Her father smiled as Jenny nodded her head eagerly and came running to his side.

"I'll do anything, Father," Jenny cried out. "Anything at all."

"Do you remember Mrs. Ross?" he asked.

"Yes, of course I do," Jenny answered. "She made Elizabeth, and earlier this year we went to visit her when her husband passed away."

"That's right," her father answered. "Well, Mrs. Ross is running the upholstery business now, and she needs some blue material. She has a special project that she is working on for some very important people. I was going to take it over to her shop myself, but with James sick, I can't get away. Do you suppose that you could take it to her?"

"Yes," Jenny answered excitedly, "I'd love to!"

"You are sure you know where the shop is?" her father asked.

"Yes," she answered, "It's on the other side of the green."

"That is a long way, Jenny. Are you sure you can walk that far?"

"Of course, Father," Jenny assured him. "After all, I'm nine years old!"

"All right then, Jenny." His voice was now more stern. "But you must make sure that it stays wrapped up. I don't want it to get dirty. Then, after you have finished, you must go straight home and explain to your mother why you are late."

Nodding, Jenny reached out and took the material that her father had carefully wrapped in brown paper. Smiling, she turned and, with proud steps, moved to the front door. As she opened it, she looked back at her father and called out, "Goodbye. I'll see you at supper."

Walking quickly up the street, she passed shop windows filled with bread, leather goods, clothing, and cooking pots. As she came to a corner and waited for a carriage to pass, she heard the bell from Independence Hall tolling out the one o'clock hour. Its ringing seemed to be urging her to hurry on with her errand.

Block after block, Jenny carried her package on her way to Mrs. Ross' shop. She stopped at the sight of a familiar, gold-colored house. It belonged to the O'Donald family, cousins of her mother. Deciding that she could spare a few minutes, Jenny opened the picket-fence gate that separated the front yard of the house from the street and ran down the stone walk and up the front steps. She knocked on the large, black front door, and moments later it was opened to reveal a plump, middle-aged woman with large eyes and wearing a bright-yellow dress.

"Well, Jenny Stuart. What in the world are you doing over in this part of town?" the woman asked.

"Hello, Cousin Martha," Jenny replied. "I am delivering some material to Mrs. Ross for my father. Is Sally at home?" Sally was Jenny's age, and the two of them played together every Sunday after church services.

"No," the woman shook her head, "Sally and her brother went downtown to see General Washington. He was supposed to speak at the main hall. Didn't you know about that?"

Shaking her head, Jenny replied, "No, I didn't. When Sally gets home, would you tell her that my father is giving me some material for a new doll's dress? I'll bring it on Sunday."

Laughing, the woman answered, "I sure will. Would you like to come in and have a glass of cider?"

"No, thank you," Jenny replied. "I've got to get to Mrs. Ross' shop and give her this fabric. Bye-bye!" And before her cousin could say another thing, Jenny turned, dashed through the gate, and ran back to the street. As she skipped along, she thought, "Sally sure is going to like my doll's new dress!"

By now, Jenny was far enough away from the down-town area that there were more homes and fewer shops. The yards were larger, and the trees more plentiful. She hadn't remembered it being this long a trip when she had ridden in her father's wagon. And the further she walked, the more tired she grew. Soon, the excitement of getting the material for Elizabeth's dress wore off, and, as the sun pounded on her head, she began to question why she had volunteered so eagerly for this long, hot trip.

"This is an awfully long walk," Jenny thought. "And I doubt there is any reason that Mrs. Ross needs this material really badly. She probably won't even use it today."

Deciding to rest a bit, Jenny stopped and sat on a small, stone wall outside a large home. Soon, a large black-and-white dog trotted up, wagging its tail. Jenny set her package to one side and motioned for the dog to sit beside her. The animal quickly accepted, jumping up and licking her on the face. For several minutes he allowed Jenny to pet him, and then he seemed to want to play. Jumping from the wall, he grabbed the package and raced down the street, looking behind him to see if Jenny would chase him.

"Wait!" Jenny yelled. "You can't have that!" Running as fast as she could, Jenny tried to catch the furry thief. But the dog stayed ahead of her. He rounded a corner by a small vegetable stand and disappeared. By the time Jenny got there, he was nowhere to be seen.

What would her father say when he found out that she had lost Mrs. Ross' material? Jenny was frantic. She ran down the street, calling for the dog, looking under every bush and behind every tree, but he was nowhere in sight. Neither was the package. Exhausted, she fell against a tree and began to cry.

After several minutes, she heard a voice ask, "What's wrong, young lady?"

Looking up, Jenny saw a man on a large, white horse. He was the same man she had seen giving a speech as she was on her way to her father's shop. Drying her eyes with the back of her hand, Jenny told her story.

"I believe I saw that dog," the man replied when she finished.

Her face brightening, Jenny asked hopefully, "Where?"

"He ran past me as I was riding up the street. But he didn't have anything in his mouth. He must have dropped your package between here and there. Come with me. We'll find your package."

Running over to him, Jenny grabbed his hand and swung up in the saddle. The man turned the horse and retraced the path he had just travelled.

The two of them searched up and down both sides of the street as the horse ambled forward. They had covered almost a block when Jenny called out, "There! Over by the bush!" Stopping his mount, the man swung Jenny to the ground and watched as she ran over to the package.

"Did the dog tear it?" the man asked.

Looking it over carefully, Jenny shook her head as she clutched the precious package to her chest. "No, only the paper. The material is fine."

"Good," the rider answered. "Now where is it you were taking it?"

"To Mrs. Ross' upholstery shop. It is right . . . ." But the man interrupted before Jenny could finish explaining.

"I was just there," he replied. "I'll give you a ride."

Within two minutes, they had covered the distance and Jenny could finally breath easier. Jumping off the horse, she thanked the man and then raced as fast as she could to the building's front door. Pushing it open, she spotted Mrs. Ross and ran over to her.

"Why, if it isn't Jenny Stuart with my blue material," the young woman said. "I need this very badly. As a matter of fact, the whole country is waiting for this fabric." Taking it from Jenny, she walked over to her sewing table and laid it next to a large red and white rectangle. "It's perfect," Mrs. Ross smiled as she compared the colors. "General Washington will be very pleased."

"General Washington!" Jenny exclaimed. "You are making something for General Washington?"

Laughing, the woman picked up a needle and began to sew. "He didn't tell you?" she asked.

Puzzled, Jenny just stared at the woman. Seeing that Jenny had not understood her teasing, Mrs. Ross added, "He was the man you were riding with just now. I assumed that you were friends."

Awestruck, Jenny turned back to the door just as the general walked in, a smile on his ruddy face. "Well, Jenny," he asked, "is Mrs. Ross satisfied with the color?"

"Yes, sir," Jenny stammered. Then, before anyone could say anything, she added, "I sure am glad that I had a chance to meet someone as important as you, General Washington, sir."

The general looked into the girl's eyes and said softly, "Jenny, you are just as important as I am."

"No sir," Jenny disagreed. "You are the man who is going to win our freedom. My father says you are the greatest man in the colonies."

Shaking his head, General Washington took Jenny's hand and led her over to Mrs. Rosses' sewing table. "Jenny, I'm only one man doing his part. All who are behind the cause of freedom are equally important. Each of us is serving his country.

"Jenny," he went on, "everyone in this country has a part to play. Old Ben Franklin, Thomas Jefferson, and a group of others are forming a government. I'm putting together an army. You delivered this material, and now Mrs. Betsy Ross is taking that material and making a symbol – a flag – that will stand for our thirteen united states. Only by your doing your job can Mrs. Ross finish hers. So, without you, our army wouldn't have a banner to represent us in battle and, someday, in peace.

"Yes, Jenny, and beyond the fact that you delivered this material, you are important because, as a person, your life will be woven into all that this flag represents."